Invisible Oink

ALSO BY LOUIS PHILLIPS

How Do You Get a Horse
out of the Bathtub?
Profound Answers to Preposterous Questions

263 Brain Busters
Just How Smart Are You, Anyway?

Sportsathon
(with Vic Braden)

Haunted House Jokes

Going Ape
Jokes From the Jungle

How Do You Lift a Walrus
with One Hand?
More Profound Answers to Preposterous Questions

Way Out!
Jokes from Outer Space

Wackysaurus
Dinosaur Jokes

Invisible Oink

PIG JOKES

By Louis Phillips
Illustrated by Arlene Dubanevich

VIKING

FOR
Morty, Rebecca, and especially Amalia,
Some jokes to enjoy far away in New Jersey
—L.P.

VIKING
Published by the Penguin Group
Penguin Books USA Inc., 375 Hudson Street, New York, New York 10014, U.S.A.
Penguin Books Ltd., 27 Wrights Lane, London W8 5TZ, England
Penguin Books Australia Ltd., Ringwood, Victoria, Australia
Penguin Books Canada Ltd., 10 Alcorn Avenue, Toronto, Ontario, Canada M4V 3B2
Penguin Books (N.Z.) Ltd., 182–190 Wairau Road, Auckland 10, New Zealand

Penguin Books Ltd., Registered Offices: Harmondsworth, Middlesex, England

First published in 1993 by Viking, a division of Penguin Books USA Inc.

1   3   5   7   9   10   8   6   4   2

LIBRARY OF CONGRESS CATALOGING-IN-PUBLICATION DATA
Phillips, Louis.
Invisible oink: pig jokes / by Louis Phillips; illustrated by Arlene Dubanevich p. cm.
Summary: A collection of anecdotes, jokes, and riddles all about pigs.
ISBN 0-670-84387-3
1. Swine—Juvenile humor.   2. Riddles—Juvenile.   3. Wit and humor, juvenile.
[I. Pigs—Wit and humor.   2. Jokes   3. riddles.]   I. Dubanevich, Arlene, III.   II. title.
PN6231.S895P45 1993   818.5402—dc20   92-24803   CIP   AC
Printed in U.S.A.
Set in 13 pt. Meridien

CONTENTS

CHAPTER ONE

Oinkers Aweigh

I Never Sausage a Collection of
Weird Pig Jokes in All My Life

ROBERT: What are some movies to show at a film festival for pigs?

DOROTHY: What?

ROBERT: *The Sty That Came In From the Cold* and *Pigmalion*.

ANNIE: What's the best way to keep a pig from smelling?

MARK: Give it a bath?

ANNIE: No. Hold its nose.

ROBERT: Why do pigs have the best writing instruments?

DORIS: Because their pens never run out of oink.

OONA: Why did the pig cross the road?

MARY ELLEN: I give up. Why?

OONA: It was the chicken's day off.

DEBORAH: What do you get when you cross a pig with vanishing cream?

LOUIS: What?

DEBORAH: Invisible oink.

PIGLET #1: Boy, it's hot today.

PIGLET #2: I never sausage heat.

PIGLET #1: Me either. I'm bacon.

PIGLET #1: Where do you bathe?

PIGLET #2: In the spring.

PIGLET #1: I said where, not when.

Knock, knock.
Who's there?
Oink, oink.
Oink, oink, who?
Make up your mind. Are you a pig or an owl?

RACHEL: What looks like half a pig?
CHAIM: Nothing.

DEBORAH: What beats chasing a pig around the yard?
RACHEL: Your heart.

RUTH: Why did the pig cross the road?
REAGAN: To prove it was not chicken.

YGGIP—Piggy back.

RACHEL: What do you call a pig who crosses the road twice but refuses to take a bath?

ADAM: What?

RACHEL: A dirty double-crosser.

PRISONER #468954: What are you doing time for?

PRISONER #579648: For stealing a pig.

PRISONER #468954: That so?

PRISONER #579648: Yes.

PRISONER #468954: How did you get caught?

PRISONER #579648: The pig squealed.

JOHN: When should you give pig milk to a baby?
KATIE: When?
JOHN: When the baby is a pig.

JOYCE: My cousin makes her living with her pen.
KAREN: You mean she writes books?
JOYCE: No. Actually, she raises pigs.

ROBERT: What's the difference between newborn pigs
   in a sty that has lots of holes in it and a play by
   Shakespeare?
DOROTHY: I give up. What?
ROBERT: One is an airy litter, while the other is literary.

DOROTHY: Here, Cotton! Here, Cotton!
ROBERT: Why do you call your pet pig Cotton?
DOROTHY: Because he shrinks from washing.

GINNY: What do you get when you cross a pig with a porcupine?
STEPHEN: What?
GINNY: A very cross pig.

What do you call very short pigs?
  Pigmies.

CUSTOMER IN RESTAURANT: Tell me, waiter, do you have pig's feet?
WAITER: No, I'm just wearing funny-looking shoes.

JOHN: What's the difference between a pig and a doughnut?

GINNY: What?

JOHN: It's a lot more difficult to dunk a pig into your coffee.

GINNY: What do you get when you cross a pig with a zebra?

STEPHEN: I give up. What?

GINNY: You get bacon with black-and-white stripes.

CHARLOTTE: What's the name of your pig?

WILLIAM: I don't know. He refuses to tell me.

PIGLET: Trouble with you is that you're way overweight.

HOG: Not true. I'm just seven inches too short.

JILL: What has a curly tail and goes *moo, moo*?
JUSTIN: What?
JILL: A very confused pig.

JAN: What weighs 10,000 pounds and goes *oink, oink*?
BILLY: Two 5,000-pound pigs.

A man is riding his horse through a small town in Missouri. He is lost, so he decides to stop and ask for directions. He spies a farmer who is walking down the road with a cute little pink pig trotting along beside him.

The man on horseback hails the farmer. "Howdy, mister."

"Howdy, stranger."

"Tell me, mister, how can I reach the Bates' farm?"

Before the farmer can answer, the cute little pink pig opens its mouth and says, "Just follow this road for three miles in the direction you are headed, turn right at Colby's General Store, go for two more miles, and you'll be right where you want to go."

The man on horseback is astounded. "Wow!" he says. "Isn't that the most amazing thing you've ever seen?"

"What's so amazing about that?" answers the farmer. "This pig has lived here all her life. She ought to be able to tell you how to get to Bates' farm."

What is the favorite movie of young pigs?
Piggy Sue Got Married.

PAUL: What is pink, has a curly tail, and sixteen
    wheels?
REAGAN: What?
PAUL: A pig on roller skates.

ROBERT: Wow, that farmer who raises pigs is a great
    magician.
DORIS: What do you mean?
ROBERT: Just the other morning he turned his pigs into
    a pen.

NANCY: Please spell *pig*.
IAN: P-I.
NANCY: But what's at the end of it?
IAN: Its tail, of course.

GRAHAM: What is pink and
    goes hop, hop, hop?
JOAN: What?
GRAHAM: A pig on a pogo stick.

PIGLET #1: The farmer wants to put a beehive near our pen.

PIGLET #2: Tell him to buzz off.

IAN: What did the pig say to the ear of corn?

PAT: What?

IAN: It's been nice gnawing you.

FARMER #1: Did you hear about the time I taught my favorite pig how to bowl?

FARMER #2: Spare me!

NOAH: What's that pig doing with a hammer?

ALEX: Don't worry. He only wants to go to sleep.

NOAH: So what does he need a hammer for?

ALEX: He's going to hit the hay.

MARK: What did the pig sing when he joined the navy?

MISSY: What?

MARK: "Oinkers aweigh, my boys/oinkers aweigh!"

DON: What's the best way to catch a pig?
COREY: Why would anyone want to catch a pig?

MATTHEW: What has horns, gives milk, and goes *oink, oink*?
IAN: I give up. What?
MATTHEW: A pig.
IAN: But pigs don't have horns and they don't give milk.
MATTHEW: I know. I added that just to make the riddle hard.

FARMER #1: That pig over there just walked through my screen door.
FARMER #2: Is he all right?
FARMER #1: Yeah. He just strained himself.

PIGLET #1: How did you happen to become the fastest pig in the barnyard?
PIGLET #2: It was easy. The farmer told me that if I ever lost a race, I would have to take a bath.

PIGLET #1: My sister fell down a flight of stairs last night and broke her leg.

PIGLET #2: Cellar?

PIGLET #1: No. The farmer said we could still keep her.

ANNIE: If a pig lost its nice curly tail, where could it get a new one?

OONA: Where?

ANNIE: At the retail shop.

FARMER #1: Boy, that was some tornado last night.

FARMER #2: Yep.

FARMER #1: Did it damage your pigpen?

FARMER #2: I don't know. I haven't found it yet.

FARMER: EEEooohh! Here, 15-Watt Light Bulb! Here, piggy, piggy, piggy.

ARNIE: Why do you call your pig 15-Watt Light Bulb?

FARMER: Because he's not very bright.

SILLY FARMER: If you can guess how many pigs I have in my sack, I'll give you both of them.

~~~~~~

A man went to the bank and took out one thousand dollars in crisp, new one-hundred-dollar bills. On the way home, he decided to go to the movies to see a science fiction movie. He sat down and placed the envelope with the thousand dollars in it on the seat beside him. Halfway through the movie, he looked over at the seat next to him and saw that a large pig had eaten his envelope.

The man became very angry and went to find the manager. "A pig got into the theater and ate an important envelope of mine," the man told the manager.

"Don't complain to me," the movie-house manager answered. "The pig belongs to the piano player who is working in the nightclub across the street."

The man stormed out of the movie theater, crossed the street, and entered the nightclub. He went up to the piano player and tapped him on the shoulder and said, "Pardon me, buddy, but do you know a pig has just eaten all of my money?"

The piano player looked at him and said, "No, but hum a few bars of it, and I'll fake it."

JUDGE: You admit, then, that you stole the farmer's pig.

DEFENDANT: Yes, Your Honor.

JUDGE: Well, there has been a lot of pig stealing lately, and I am going to make an example of you, or none of us will be safe.

NANCY: Be nice to me. I just defended you.

LAUREN: How?

NANCY: That boy over there said you weren't fit to live with the pigs, and I said you were.

CHAPTER TWO

The Most Boaring Chapter in Joke-Book History

*But If You Skip It You Will Be
Making a Pig Mistake!*

ANDY: I just shot a boar and a potfer.
SUE: What's a potfer?
ANDY: To cook the boar in, silly.

What do wild pigs in France serve with their dinners?
Boar-deaux wine, of course.

What kind of snakes do wild pigs fear the most?
Boar constrictors.

Where do wild pigs stay when they visit the city?
In boar-ding houses, of course.

What wild pig goes around stamping out forest fires?
Smokey the Boar.

What was the name of the wild pig that went around poisoning all of her relatives?
Lucretia Boar-gia.

What wild pig was a famous movie star in the film Casablanca?

Humphrey Boar-Gart.

What country has more wild pigs than any other?

Boar-neo.

What is the favorite story of wild pigs?

"Goldilocks and the Three Boars."

Why did the three little pigs run away from home?

Their father was a dreadful boar.

ELYSA: What do you call a boar who has more than one wife?

JENNIFER: I give up. What?

ELYSA: A pigamist.

Where do wild pigs go for their vacations?
They usually go to the South Pacific island of Boara-Boara (Bora-Bora).

BOAR #1: I was born in Bora-Bora.
BOAR #2: What part?
BOAR #1: Why, all of me, of course.

JOHN: Did you hear about the wild boar that tried to swim the English channel?
KATIE: No. What happened?
JOHN: The wild boar swam halfway across, decided it was too far to go, and so he swam back.

KATIE: Why did the boar slide down the chimney?
JOHN: I don't know.
KATIE: Someone told him he needed a new soot.

MORTY: Look at that bunch of boars!

HUNTER: That's not a bunch of boars. It's a herd.

MORTY: Heard what?

HUNTER: Herd of boars.

MORTY: Of course I've heard of a bunch of boars. I pointed them out to you, didn't I?

HUNTER: No, no. You mean a boar-herd.

MORTY: Why should I care what a wild pig heard?

HUNTER: Heard what?

MORTY: Forget it. Just tell me, what do you call a boar's skin?

HUNTER: Hide!

MORTY: Hide? Why should I hide?

HUNTER: Hide, hide, the boar's outside.

MORTY: So what if it's outside? I'm not scared.

HUNTER: I give up!

Who is a wild boar's favorite skater?
   Piggy Fleming.

PIG #1: Stay away from that boar over there.

PIG #2: Why?

PIG #1: Because he is one really tough animal.

PIG #2: How tough?

PIG #1: He's so tough he uses barbed wire for dental floss.

JOHN: Why did the baby boar stuff his father into the freezer?

KATIE: I give up. Why?

JOHN: Because it was summer and he wanted some frozen pop.

What game do baby boars play with their parents?
Pig-a-boo.

Who is the favorite painter of boars?
Pig-casso.

Who was the favorite silent-screen movie star of boars?
Mary Pigford.

What is the favorite old song of boars?
"Pig o' My Heart."

MARY ELLEN: Why are wild pigs the dullest of all
animals?
CAROLINE: I give up. Why?
MARY ELLEN: Because they are all boars (bores).

CAROLINE: If ten boars run after two boars, what time
is it?
HELEN: I don't know. What time is it?
CAROLINE: Ten after two.

BOAR #1: I can see that you're the kind of wild pig who does a lot of traveling.

BOAR #2: I do, but how could you possibly tell?

BOAR #1: By the bags under your eyes.

BOB: I had wild boar for lunch.

MARGIE: Was it really wild?

BOB: Well, it wasn't very pleased.

CHARLES: Did you hear what happened when a herd of wild boar ran through the cows' milking shed?

CAROLINE: No. What happened?

CHARLES: There was udder chaos.

PIG (to a large boar that has just run him over): Say, it's not necessary to knock me down like that, is it?

BOAR: Of course not.

PIG: I thought not.

BOAR: Just get up and let me show you ten other ways to do it.

CHAPTER THREE

Hamming It Up

CUSTOMER IN RESTAURANT: How do you account for the fact that I found a piece of rubber in one of the ham steaks?

WAITER: I guess that came from the pig that was run over by a truck.

NICHOLAS: Who is the favorite president of pigs?
JOHN: Abra*ham* Lincoln.

ANNETTE: Where do hogs go when they vacation in Germany?
HENRY: *Ham*burg, of course.

CUSTOMER IN RESTAURANT: Excuse me, but what dish am I eating?
WAITER: Cold boiled ham.
CUSTOMER: What is cold boiled ham? I never heard of such a thing.
WAITER: Why, madam, it is merely ham boiled in cold water.

CUSTOMER IN RESTAURANT: Excuse me, but how was this ham prepared?
WAITER: It was smothered in onions.
CUSTOMER: Well, the pig sure died hard.

CUSTOMER IN RESTAURANT: Waiter!
WAITER: Yes, sir?
CUSTOMER: There's not much ham in this ham sandwich.
WAITER: How do you know, sir?
CUSTOMER: A little swallow told me.

CUSTOMER IN RESTAURANT: Let me have some ham. Cut
it thin. An eighth of an inch thick. Don't turn it over.
Not too much fat. Just two pinches of salt. A pinch of
pepper. Cook for exactly eight minutes. Add parsley.
Well? What are you waiting for?

WAITER: The pig's name was Harvey. Is that all right,
sir?

RACHEL: In the Old Testament, who was the pig's
favorite person?

DEBORAH: Who?

RACHEL: The answer is obvious—Noah's son, Ham.

LOU: What is the favorite play of pigs?

LILLIAN: *Ham*let.

What do you call non-professional hogs?
*Ham*ateurs.

What do you call a hog that can use all its legs with equal skill?
*Ham*bidextrous.

What do you use to take a sick pig to the hospital?
A *ham*bulance.

Where do Texas pigs go for a vacation?
They go to *Ham*arillo.

What pig was vice-president of the United States under Abraham Lincoln?
Hannibal *Ham*lin.

What hog served as secretary-general of the United Nations from 1953 to 1961?
Dag *Ham*marskjold.

How does Miss Piggy travel to work?
By *Ham*trak.

What do you call a person who breaks into pigpens and steals pigs?
  A *ham*burglar.

What pig wrote the most music for Broadway musicals?
  Oscar *Ham*merstein II.

Where do hogs go in the summertime?
  New *Ham*pshire.

PAT: What do pigs sleep in?
MATTHEW: I don't know. In what?
PAT: *Ham*mocks.

AMY: What do you call a pig who is related to
  Dracula?
IAN: What?
AMY: A *ham*pire.

NICK: What river do pigs sail down in South America?
CHRISTINE: The *Ham*azon river, of course.

What do you call pigs sent on a diplomatic mission to foreign countries?
  *Ham*bassadors.

A BRIEF THOUGHT ABOUT THE STEALING OF
PIGS IN A CERTAIN COUNTY IN GEORGIA
  The bacon
  In Macon
  Is not for the takin'.

MARGIE: What do you get if you cross an owl with a lazy hog?

BOB: What?

MARGIE: An animal that doesn't give a hoot about bringing home the bacon.

SUE: What is the only animal that is killed before it is cured?

ANDY: What?

SUE: The pig.

Chapter Four

Sunday in the Pork with George

MRS. STONE: Where do pigs go when they visit New York City?

IAN: The answer is obvious. They go to Central Pork.

NANCY: What do you call it when a pig takes up karate?

DON: Pork chop.

WOMAN AT THE BUTCHER SHOP: I want to buy some pork chops.

BUTCHER: Certainly, ma'am.

WOMAN: And I'll have the pork chops lean.

BUTCHER: Certainly, ma'am. In which direction?

BOB: What do pigs wear in Alaska?

KAY: They wear porkas (parkas).

MARY: What's the difference between a place that sells pigs and a slice of roasted pig?

JONATHAN: One's a pork shop, while the other is a pork chop.

LORNA: Did you see those pigs rooting through the garbage?

LESLIE: Oh, don't talk rubbish.

Who is the favorite baseball player of pigs?
Dave Porker.

What is pink, has warts, and lights up?
An electric warthog.

GINNY: What do you get when you cross a pig, a sheep, and a fir tree?

STEPHEN: I give up. What?

GINNY: A pork-ewe-pine.

CUSTOMER IN RESTAURANT: Waiter! This pork chop I ordered is very small.

WAITER: I know, madam, but don't complain. You got your money's worth.

CUSTOMER: How?

WAITER: The pork chop may be small, but it's so tough that it will take you at least an hour to chew it.

ANDY: Who is Porky Pig's favorite poet?

SUE: I give up. Who is it?

ANDY: Hogden Nash.

Why did the pig get a ticket when he drove his car to town?
    He forgot to put money in the porking meter.

CUSTOMER IN RESTAURANT: Waiter! There's a piece of
wood in my pork chop.

WAITER: I'm sorry, sir . . . but . . .

CUSTOMER: *But* nothing. I don't mind eating the pork
chop, but I refuse to eat the pigpen, too.

MORTY: Why are pigs such bad dancers?

AMALIA: Because they have two left feet.

MAC: Which Broadway musical do pigs prefer above
all others?

BOB: I don't know. What Broadway musical *do* pigs
prefer above all others?

MAC: *Sunday in the Pork with George.*

Two minor league teams were playing a game far out in the country in a field owned by a pig farmer. In the bottom of the ninth, the batter hit the ball into the pig sty and the pig ate the baseball, allowing the winning run to score. It was the first occurrence of an inside-the-pork home run.

Chapter Five

Hog Wild

CITY SLICKER: Hey, Mr. Farmer, do you have any wild hogs?

FARMER: No, but I can give you a tame one and you can get him mad.

HOG #1: I run all day long, I run and I run and I run, but I move only four feet.

HOG #2: Why? Because you're so fat?

HOG #1: No. Those are all the feet I have.

CUSTOMER IN RESTAURANT: Waiter! What is this hog doing in my soup?

WAITER: Sorry, sir. It was the fly's day off.

ARNIE: Why shouldn't you allow male pigs to play basketball?

SAM: Why?

ARNIE: Because they always hog the ball.

Why do hogs hate to go to football games?
They can't stand to see players tossing the old pigskin
around.

HOG #1: Did you take a bath?
HOG #2: Why? Is there one missing?

THE ANSWER IS: HOGWASH
*THE QUESTION IS: What do you call a pig's underwear
hanging on the clothesline?*

HOG #1: Shall we shoo the flies?
HOG #2: Naah. Let them go barefoot.

HOG #1: Are you certain that all the corn has been
eaten?
HOG #2: I *know* all the corn has been eaten.
HOG #1: How do you know?
HOG #2: I have inside information.

A farmer was walking down a dirt road with two very beautiful hogs under his arm, when a man named Jeb stopped him.

"Hey, stranger, where are you going with those two hogs?" Jeb asked the farmer.

"Oh, I'm just taking them out for a breath of early morning air."

"That's nice."

"Yes, it is."

"Tell me, stranger," Jeb continued. "Those are two of the most beautiful, well-fed hogs I have ever seen. How can you raise them like that?"

"It's easy," said the farmer. "Every day at five in the morning, I get up, put one hog under one arm, one hog under my other arm, and we go out for a ten-mile hike to the apple orchard on top of the hill over there. I lift one hog up to take an apple from the branch, and then I lift the other hog up to eat a fresh apple, and that's what I do until the hogs aren't hungry anymore. And then I carry them home."

"Doesn't that take a lot of time?"

"Yep," the farmer said, "but what's time to a hog?"

ARTIST #1: Here is my famous painting of five hogs at the feeding trough eating mash and corn.

ARTIST #2: But I don't see the mash and corn in the trough.

ARTIST #1: The hogs ate it all.

ARTIST #2: But I don't see the five hogs, either.

ARTIST #1: Well, of course not.

ARTIST #2: Why *of course not?*

ARTIST #1: Why should the hogs stay around after all the food has been eaten?

IVY: What do you call a hog at the North Pole?

FIFI: I'd call it one very lost hog.

BOB: Who is the hog's favorite character in American history?

DORIS: Who?

BOB: Oinkle Sam.

HOG #1: I went to the veterinarian yesterday.
HOG #2: Does your tooth still ache?
HOG #1: I don't know. He kept it.

THE ANSWER IS: HOG WILD.
THE QUESTION IS: What is the
value of the hog card in a game of poker?

PAUL: What's a hammock?
REGAN: When you make fun of a hog?

A little girl was holding the leash on a 500-pound hog
going down the road.
FARMER: Where are you going?
LITTLE GIRL: I'm going to go wherever *he* wants to go!

HOG #1: Hey! What should I do if I break my leg in
two places?
HOG #2: Don't go back to those places again.

TOM: Where do hogs in Alaska live?
JONATHAN: In pigloos.

PIGLET: Dad, how many ears of corn could you eat on
an empty stomach?
FATHER HOG: Only one.
PIGLET: How come? I thought hogs were supposed to
have great appetites.
FATHER HOG: True, but after I eat one ear of corn, my
stomach won't be empty anymore.

HOG #1: Did you hear what happened to me last month? Two hunters thought I was a deer and accidentally shot me in the leg.

HOG #2: Have a scar?

HOG #1: No, thank you. I don't smoke.

TEACHER: Now, Matthew, if Lauren gave you a hog, and Nancy gave you another hog, how many hogs would you have?

MATTHEW: Six hogs.

TEACHER: Now, Matthew, use your head. Try again. If Lauren gave you a hog, and Nancy gave you another hog, how many hogs would you have?

MATTHEW: Six hogs. You see, I already own four hogs!

PIGLET: Mommy, how come my snout is in the middle of my face?

MOTHER HOG: Because it's a scenter.

FARMER BRODIE: What do you think of that 1,000-pound hog over there?

FARMER PHILLIPS: Wow! I never sausage a hog!

A farmer was playing chess with his favorite hog when a reporter happened upon the scene.

REPORTER: Wow! Is this a big story! I have never seen a hog play chess before. That hog must be very clever.

FARMER: Not so clever.

REPORTER: Why not?

FARMER: Because I have beaten him three out of four so far.

SAM: In Scotland, why is the night before New Year's Day the favorite holiday of pigs?

FAY: Why?

SAM: Because in Scotland, New Year's Eve is called *Hog*manay.

What do you get if you cross a hog with a kangaroo and a loaf of bread?

A ham sandwich in pocket bread.

NICHOLAS: What's the difference between an animal that emerges from underground to see its shadow every February and a sausage?

JENNIFER: What?

NICHOLAS: One is a groundhog, while the other is ground hog.

I never sausage a shadow!

ARNIE: When I do my hog calls, people clap their hands.

NANCY: Yes. Over their ears.

MARY: A hog wanted to cross a river to eat the corn in the cornfield, but there was no bridge across the river, no boat, and the hog couldn't swim. So how did the pig get across the river?

JONATHAN: I don't know.

MARY: You give up?

JONATHAN: Yes.

MARY: So did the hog.

BOB: I was at the 4-H fair the other day.

KAY: So?

BOB: I saw a hog almost as big as an elephant. I never saw such a hog.

KAY: I believe you.

ALEX: Tell that old hog to get off the kitchen stove.

NOAH: Why?

ALEX: Because he's too old to ride the range.

MARK: Why do hogs lie down in the mud?
HILDA: Because they cannot lie up in it.

JANEY: What do hogs study in school?
ROSS: What?
JANEY: *Pen*manship and *Litter*ature.

RECKLESS DRIVER: Gee, I'm awfully sorry. I just ran over your hog.
IRATE FARMER: You ran over my hog?
RECKLESS DRIVER: Don't worry. I'll replace it!
IRATE FARMER: What good will that do? I can't get ham and bacon from you!

VIRGINIA: What happened to the 1,000-pound hog that crashed through the floor of the theater?
AMY: What?
VIRGINIA: Nothing. It was just a stage it was going through.

CHAPTER SIX

Tales (and Tails) from
A Sows and One Nights

What is the favorite storybook of a pig?
The Arabian collection of tales called *A Sows and One Nights*.

FARMER: The sow in the pen is running a high temperature.
FARMER'S WIFE: How high?
FARMER: Two bales.
FARMER'S WIFE: Two bales? That's no way to take a pig's temperature.
FARMER: Of course it is. She has hay fever.

SOW: What's the matter, Son? You look mournful.
PIGLET: That's just the trouble, Mom. I'm more 'n full.

FARMER: How much do you think that 100-pound sow weighs?
FARMHAND: I don't know.
FARMER: Let me give you a hint. What year did the War of 1812 start?
FARMHAND: 1812.
FARMER: So, use your head. How much does that 100-pound sow weigh?
FARMHAND: Oh, it's easy. Between 12 and 18 pounds.

SOW #1: Do you get enough iron in your diet?
SOW #2: I chew my nails.

ANNIE: I just lost my pet sow.
OONA: Did you put an ad in the newspaper?
ANNIE: Naah. She can't read.

MOTHER SOW: When you saw Junior drinking ink, why didn't you do something?
SISTER: I did. I made him eat a blotter.

SOW #1: It must be early morning.
SOW #2: How do you know?
SOW #1: It just dawned on me.

SOW #1: Look at the sunset in the west.
SOW #2: So what? I've got a son so lazy that he rises early in the morning and sets all day.

HOG: Marry me, darling, and I'll make you the happiest sow in all the fifty states.
SOW: No, thanks. I don't want to live in a trailer.

BOB: I hope you put snew in the pigpen. Sows love snew.
DORIS: Snew? What's snew?
BOB: Nothing. What's new with you?

LORNA: That sow is a pet. She's just like one of the family.

LESLIE: Yes, but which one?

SOW #1: Listen to the farmer. He whistles while he works.

SOW #2: He must be happy.

SOW #1: No. He has gaps in his teeth.

SOW #1: I don't like corn and I am glad that I don't like it.

SOW #2: Why?

SOW #1: Because if I did like it, I would eat it, and I hate the stuff.

JACKIE: How are two sows on a fence like a penny?

MICHAEL: I don't know. How?

JACKIE: Heads on one side, tails on the other.

SOW: What would you do if the pigpen caught fire?
PIGLET: I'd shout.
SOW: Yes, but what would you shout?
PIGLET: Cease fire!

HOG #1: That sow over there doesn't seem very intelligent.
HOG #2: I know. She hasn't paid any attention to me, either.

HOG: You know your head reminds me of a classic story?
SOW: I know. *Sleeping Beauty.*
HOG: No. *The Legend of Sleepy Hollow.*

BOB: What do you call a sow that has been smoked and cured?
MARGIE: I don't know. What?
BOB: Dinner.

SOW #1: Do you think I should have my singing voice cultivated?
SOW #2: Perhaps you should think about having it plowed under.

What was the female pig's favorite movie?
Peggy Sow Got Married.

What was the name of the sow who campaigned for the right of women to vote?
*Sow*san B. Anthony.

PIGLET: Mom, I think we're lost.

SOW: What makes you think so?

PIGLET: I hear savage cries and the natives are beating their clubs on the ground.

SOW: Ah! It just means we're nearing the golf course.

VIRGINIA: I know a farmer who loves wool but hates sheep.

COREY: What's he going to do?

VIRGINIA: He's going to develop a special kind of sow that grows wool and then when the sows are eating from the trough, he'll cut the wool off. What do you think of that?

COREY: I think it's sheer nonsense.

CHAPTER SEVEN

Piglets on Parade

PIGLET #1: Can you stand on your head?

PIGLET #2: No. It's too high.

ANNIE: What happened to the piglet when she fell into a pile of feathers?

OONA: I imagine she was tickled pink.

FARMER IN THE DELL: Was that soil you bought for the pigpen expensive?

FARMER IN THE DELI: No. In fact, it was dirt cheap.

PIGLET #1: My grandfather was the first hog on this farm to take a milk bath.

PIGLET #2: Really?

PIGLET #1: Yes. His bath lasted ten years.

PIGLET #2: Why? Was he that dirty?

PIGLET #1: No. He had trouble getting the milk out of the carton.

PIGLET #1: Whatever I do, I do the best way I know how.

PIGLET #2: Really?

PIGLET #1: Yes. Whatever I do, I throw myself into my work.

PIGLET #2: Did you ever try digging a well?

PIGLET #1: How many times have I told you not to tell me secrets in the cornfield?

PIGLET #2: Why not?

PIGLET #1: Because the corn has ears.

PIGLET #1: When's your birthday?

PIGLET #2: March 17.

PIGLET #1: What year?

PIGLET #2: Every year, silly.

What popular game do piglets play?
Pig-up sticks.

～～～～～～～～～～～～～～～～～

The three little pigs were busy building their houses. The little pig who was building his house out of wood kept picking up nails, looking at them, and then throwing some of the nails away. The pig who was building his house out of brick could not help but notice the strange behavior of his younger brother, so he went over and asked him, "Why are you throwing these nails away? They're perfectly good nails."

"No, they're not," the younger brother said. "Can't you see that their points are all facing in the wrong direction?"

PIGLET #1: It's going to be summer soon.
PIGLET #2: How do you know?
PIGLET #1: I can see the popsicle trucks heading north.

PIGLET #1: What's that ugly sow doing in the pigpen?

PIGLET #2: That ugly sow you're talking about happens to be my sister!

PIGLET #1: Sorry. Ah! Now I see the resemblance.

PIGLET #1: Boy. It's sure dark in this barn.

PIGLET #2: How can you tell? I can't see a thing.

PIGLET #1: Boy, it's hot today.

PIGLET #2: I never sausage heat.

PIGLET #1: Me either. I'm bacon.

PIGLET #1: There are two things I never eat for breakfast.

PIGLET #2: What's that? Corn and mash?

PIGLET #1: No. Lunch and dinner.

CHRISTIAN: What happened to the mother pig when she left all her little piglets in the middle of the sidewalk?

IAN: I give up. What happened?

CHRISTIAN: She was fined for littering.

A piglet was standing in the middle of a field, going moo, moo, *when his mother came over to him.*

MOTHER: What are you doing? Pigs go *oink, oink,* not *moo, moo.*

PIGLET: I know, Mother, but I thought it was time for me to learn a foreign language.

PIGLET #1: The farmer is going to take me to market on a boat.

PIGLET #2: So?

PIGLET #1: So I'm afraid I'm going to get seasick. I've never been seasick before. What will I do?

PIGLET #1: Don't worry. You'll do it.

JOHN: When piglets write letters, to whom do they write?

ANDY: I guess they write to their pen pals.

PIGLET #1: I'm glad I'm not a bird.
PIGLET #2: Why not?
PIGLET #1: Because I can't fly.